A Christmas to Remember

I'm Dreaming Of A White Christmas

D. Morgan

HARVEST HOUSE PUBLISHERS
EUGENE, OREGON 97402

DEDICATION

To the loving memory of my son, Dutch Whitten Cofer, whose brief candle burned only half a lifetime, but with twice the light.

and...

To the loving memory of my daddy, John Lovic Whitten, a genteel country gentleman, an artist with the sensitivity of Robert Frost and the patience of Job.

A CHRISTMAS TO REMEMBER

There's a glow in early evening
Soft as lantern light.
The purple shadows falling
Like a fragile paper kite.

The air, crisp as apples
Makes hurried steps so light
And in the sounds of silence
There is magic in the night.

D. MORGAN

With snow upon our window ~ a crackling fire inside ~ we'

..... And hitch the horse ..... for a Winter's

Ev

Diana's cousins, the Murr

Anne revell

heat the brick . . . . .

Sleigh ride :

. . . om Newbridge, came; they all crowded in the big sleigh, among straw and funny robes.

. . . the drive to the hall, slipping along over the satin-smoothed roads with the snow crisping under the runners . . . .

Tinkles of sleigh bells and distant laughter, that seemed like the mirth of wood elves, came from every quarter.

LUCY MAUD MONTGOMERY – *Anne of Green Gables*

D. Morgan © 1996

THE SHEPHERDS AND THE ANGELS

That night some shepherds were in the fields outside the village, guarding their flocks of sheep.

Suddenly an angel appeared among them…. He said, "I bring you the most joyful news ever

announced, and it is for everyone! The Savior…has been born tonight in Bethlehem!"

"He will be the greatest joy of many…and the deepest thoughts of many hearts shall be revealed."

THE BOOK OF LUKE

charm of the wide

I remember the softness and

of August. And in winter

D. Morgan ©

Over the river and through the wood, to grandmother's house we go!

The horse knows the way, to carry the sleigh, through the white and drifted snow.

Over the river and through the wood, oh how the wind does blow!

It stings the toes and bites the nose as over the ground we go.

LYDIA MARIA CHILD

y street.

The giant tree that hung heavy with the heat

...... the warm contentment. I love remembering the simple pleasures of my grandmother's house.

I'm coming home for Christmas.

Light the candles on the tree

..... And set a place for me.

Put the cinnamon in the cider, —— the

—— I need to

...t the picture albums ......

...rs in the stew.

... my dearest memories

...e at Home With You.

D. Morgan © 1995

Christmas... is not an external event at all,

but a piece of one's home that one carries

in one's heart: like a nursery story,

its validity rests on exact repetition,

so that it comes around every time as the

evocation of one's whole life and particularly

of the most distant bits of it in childhood.

FREYA STARK

WINTERSET

Winterset has come to stay

Brush the crumbs

From hearth away.

    Settle in—

Read that book

       Perhaps

To learn again to cook.

Ponder all the dreams you may

Winterset

   Has

     Come

       To

         Stay.

D. MORGAN

Winterset

Our hearts are warm
The fire's aglow
Soup's in the kettle
Let It Snow
Let It Snow

D. Morgan ©1996

Ambrosia. What a lovely word.

A mixture, a potpourri of gastronomic pleasure. My daddy's

delectable ambrosia, which he made every Christmas Eve.

First, the coconuts. They had to be fresh. Daddy knew just how

to choose them, shaking their hairy monkey faces close to his ear.

This time-consuming ritual never seemed to be a chore for him.

Daddy had a talent for finding pleasure in the moment.

He would break open the coconuts, pouring the milk into

a glass for me. Then he would cut the coconut meat from the

shell and grate it by hand. Then came the perfect oranges.

Each one was peeled and sectioned as the bowl caught the juices.

Every seed was removed. I loved sharing the ritual with him.

It was years after he was gone before I could enjoy ambrosia

at Christmas again, and it has never been quite the same.

Ambrosia is truly for remembrance.

D. MORGAN

...C

D. Morgan © 1998

Ambrosia for remembrance brings an angel to retrieve...

my invisible keepsakes

Every Christmas Eve.

Now join your hands, and with your hands your hearts.
SHAKESPEARE

It's a holiday fraught with peril.

So achingly beautiful, with the lights twinkling and the choirs singing and

the glorious story about the Child and the shepherds kneeling in the stable,

and our hearts are open, full of generous and graceful feelings....

It's conditioning.

When you're a little kid, Christmas is imprinted on you,

and although you may rebel against old customs later and switch from

turkey to blackened redfish and decide that instead of Christmas carols

you will hold hands with each other and breathe in unison—

Christmas still lives deep in the cockles of your heart.

GARRISON KEILLOR

Jack Frost Nipping At Your Nose. D. Morgan© 1994

They go round carol-singing regularly at this time of year. They're quite an institution in these parts. And they never pass me over—they come to Mole End last of all; and I used to give them hot drinks, and supper too sometimes, when I could afford it. It will be like old times to hear them again.

KENNETH GRAHAME
The Wind in the Willows

The music plays,
The heart remembers,
And the melody
Lingers on.
D. MORGAN

D. Morgan © 1996

Folks Dressed Up Like Eskimos.

There was not a prouder nor a happier boy

in all Holland than Hans Brinker, as he watched

his sister Gretel, with many a dexterous sweep,

flying in and out among the skaters who at

sundown thronged the canal...As the little creature

darted backward and forward, flushed with

enjoyment, and quite unconscious of the

many wondering glances bent upon her,

she felt that the shining runners beneath her

feet had suddenly turned earth into Fairyland.

MARY MAPES DODGE
Hans Brinker

In our home, 'round our hearth

May there be love and laughter—

With guardian angels here to keep us

Now and ever after.

D. MORGAN

The tree made a path of ribbons

.....Heavy with chi

The smell of fresh cut pine

Each Dec

And my heart holds most d

he snow ......

D. Morgan © 1987

lights and old ornaments,
led with the aromas from the kitchen.
I think of it ~
hat beautiful Christmas memory.

We've been awhile awandering amongst the leaves so green—

But now we come awassailing, So plainly to be seen;

For it's Christmas time, when we do travel far and near;

May God bless you and send you a happy New Year.

R. VAUGHAN WILLIAMS—*Traditional Yorkshire Carol*

THE SNOWMAN

Come in the garden

And play in the snow,

A snowman we'll make,

See how quickly he'll grow!

Give him hat, stick, and pipe,

And make him look gay,

Such a fine game

For a cold winter day!

E. M. ADAMS

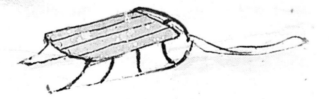

Dont look for cherubs playing harps golden

— But consider the unlikel

We never had a Christmas tree in our house. Mama would usually cook an old hen or rooster, and Lula or Mintie would bake a layer cake and put the layers together with homemade jelly. Papa would try to go to town before Christmas and get a few apples, but often he didn't make it. There was always a Christmas tree at the schoolhouse, and we had a little program every year. We didn't expect any toys. Usually, the teacher would put a little bit of candy on the tree for the little ones.

...inged and crowned —

....there are angels, all around.

D. Morgan ©1993

...manger...

One Christmas, as we were entering the building for the program, two little girls came up to me and said, "Oh, you should see what's on the tree for you." They pulled me in and showed me. There on the tree was a beautiful little basket filled with candy. I couldn't believe my eyes that it had my name on it. It was from a lady in the neighborhood that we hardly knew. I guess she admired my family, because my parents always tried to teach us to do right. Anyway, that lady could never know how much happiness she gave one little girl.

ELLA JOSEPHINE VAUSE CHRISTIAN

THE WAY IS LONG

The Way is long,

The air is cold,

But, my heart is warm,

For in a few moments…

I'll

Be

Home.

D. MORGAN

Whatever else be lost among the years,

Let us keep Christmas still a shining thing;

Whatever doubts assail us, or what fears,

Let us hold close one day, remembering

Its poignant meaning for the hearts of men.

Let us get back our childlike faith again.

GRACE NOLL CROWELL

I'm Dreaming Of A White Christmas

D. Morgan ©1997

The young ladies

decked the little fir tree out. On one branch they hung little nets cut

out of colored paper—every net was filled with sweetmeats; golden apples and

walnuts hung down as if they grew there; and more than a hundred little candles,

red, white, and blue, were fastened to the different boughs. Dolls that looked

exactly like real people—the Tree had never seen such before—swung upon the

foliage, and high on the summit of the Tree was fixed a tinsel star.

It was splendid, particularly beautiful.

HANS CHRISTIAN ANDERSEN
The Fir Tree

Gather 'round the table—all join hands in love. D. MORGAN

Yet the old house, the room,

the merry voices and smiling faces, the jest, the laugh,

the most minute and trivial circumstances connected with

those happy meetings, crowd upon our mind at each

recurrence of the season, as if the last assemblage had been

but yesterday! Happy, happy Christmas, that can win us

back to the delusions of our childish days, that can recall

to the old man the pleasures of his youth.

CHARLES DICKENS

D. Morgan © 1998

Chestnuts Roasting On An Open Fire

D. Morgan © 1993

Now all our neighbors' chimneys smoke,

And Christmas logs are burning;

Their ovens with baked meats do choke,

And all their spits are turning.

Without the door let sorrow lie,

And if for cold it hap to die,

We'll bury it in Christmas pie,

And evermore be merry!

GEORGE WITHER

Make the moments matter, for the memories you give will be with them forever—

As long as they may live.

D. MORGAN

From the morning light ... to setting sun, an angels' work is never done.

Daddy cut that pretty little pine out back.

Pulling the tree, we walked toward the house singing our funny songs.

The tree made a path of ribbons in the snow.

Mother had all the Christmas decorations unpacked and ready.

The aromas from the kitchen mingled with the freshly cut pine,

and after supper the three of us trimmed the tree.

We were careful handling the clunky lights. If one went out, so did they all.

Some ornaments were shaped like stars, some like icicles,

and there were those like winter houses with colored cellophane windows.

All were topped with white and silver sparkling glitter that shed under the tree.

When the lights caught the tiny dots, they flashed like diamonds.

From my bed, I watched the silent snow drift by my window.

Sleep came as the lights grew dim, then dark.

Each December I think of that day into evening,

and hold most dear to my heart that beautiful Christmas.

D. MORGAN

through watchful care — we have a guardian angel there.

With every step...

D. Morgan © 1994

There's a little bit of heaven
'Round the corner,
Take a right.   A cozy little cottage
With a little
Kitchen light.   A refuge when I'm weary—
A comfort when I'm blue—

There's a little bit of heaven
Coming
Home
To
You.

D. MORGAN

©1988 *D. Morgan*

Already the children were making merry. Unchecked by any frowning elder, a boisterous game of hoodman blind was in full swing, and youngsters were burning their fingers at snapdragon or sousing their heads playing bob-apple. And so with games and dancing the evening wore away, until the butler staggered in under a great bowl of wassail, from which a spicy steam wreathed up. Then came more dancing and games and singing.... A guest did not get up to go, nor a sleepy child submit to being led away, until the bells chimed out for Christmas morning.

ALISTER BURFORD

You merry folk, be of good cheer,

For Christmas comes but once a year.

From open door you'll take no harm

By winter if your hearts are warm.

GEOFFREY SMITH

REMEMBER

My heart recalls

A childhood December—

A magical time,

So

Sweet

To

Remember.

D. MORGAN

The things we do at Christmas are touched

with a certain extravagance, as beautiful, in some of its aspects,

as the extravagance of Nature in June.

ROBERT COLLYER

One doesn't forget the rounded wonder in

the eyes of a boy as he comes bursting upstairs on Christmas

morning and finds the two-wheeler or fire truck

of which for weeks he scarcely dared dream.

MAX LERNER

And in all this cold Decembering—A gentle time for sweet remembering.

D. MORGAN

SWEET REMEMBERING

CHRISTMAS PARTY

Who can be insensible to the outpourings of good feeling,

and the honest interchange of affectionate attachment,

which abound at this season of the year? A Christmas family party!

We know nothing in nature more delightful!

There seems a magic in the very name of Christmas.

CHARLES DICKENS

Yes, Virginia, there is a Santa Claus. He exists as certainly as love and generosity and devotion exist,

and you know that they abound and give to our life its highest beauty and joy.

FRANCIS P. CHURCH

Dear Santa,

Are you still the same dear man I knew so long ago

I knew the bells on reindeer hoof — and felt the snow crunch on my
How marvelously jolly round — you stilled my heart without a sound.
Now with values rearranged, pl
Does Mrs. Claus still mend y
Are you still the
I knew so .

Does Mrs. Claus still mend your suit.........

and pack your bag to go?

I ran to peek in at the tree — (that breathless little child was me.)
r quiet you were beside the tree — You drank the cocoa there from me.
don't tell me you have changed.
it and pack your bag to go?
dear man.....
go?   © 1987 D. Morgan

Guardian angels

..... with hearts

full of mercy ~ and

above .....

full of love .

D. Morgan © 1993

Blow, bugles of battle, the marches of peace;

East, west, north, and south let the long quarrel cease;

Sing the song of great joy that the angels began,

Sing the glory of God and of good-will to man!

JOHN GREENLEAF WHITTIER

Suddenly a great company of the heavenly host appeared praising God and saying,

"Glory to God in the highest, and on earth peace to men on whom his favor rests."

THE BOOK OF LUKE

Here the home fires
Burning bright
Warmed me on a winters' night
Monopoly ~
Ice cream snow ~
The Lone Ranger on the radio
Fireflies inside Mason jars ~
Swings on porches
And
Knee
Action
Cars.

Friendly neighbors
Crowleys' store.
That wonderful hat
My
Daddy
Wore.

Always in April ~   All through December...
...These were the times I love
To
Remember.

D. Morgan © 1998

MORE TO CHRISTMAS

There's more, much more, to Christmas

Than candlelight and cheer;

It's the spirit of sweet friendship

That brightens all the year;

It's thoughtfulness and kindness,

It's hope reborn again,

For peace, for understanding

And for goodwill to men!

ANONYMOUS

I do hope your Christmas has had a little touch of Eternity in among the rush and pitter patter and all. It always seems such a mixing of this world and the next—but that after all is the idea!

EVELYN UNDERHILL

May the light of Christmastide

Shed its cheering ray

O'er thy homestead,

With thee every day.

E. A. KNIGHT